Sofia the First

The Missing Necklace

Based on the episode "The Amulet of Avalor"
by Laurie Israel and Rachel Ruderman

Adapted by Lisa Ann Marsoli

Illustrated by Character Building Studio
and the Disney Storybook Art Team

DISNEP PRESS
New York • Los Angeles

First Edition   5 7 9 10 8 6
ISBN 978-1-4231-7164-5

G658-7729-4-15159

Library of Congress Control Number: 2014936780
Manufactured in the USA
For more Disney Press fun, visit www.disneybooks.com

There is going to be a ball!
Sofia gets ready.

"I have a surprise!" says King Roland.
"Follow me."

He takes Sofia and Amber to the
Jewel Room.
"Pick out something!" he says.

A baby griffin watches over
the jewels.
Griffins are part lion and part bird.
They love shiny things!

The sisters go to Sofia's room.
The griffin follows.

"Let's try on our jewels," says Amber.
Sofia takes off her necklace.

She does not see the griffin.
He flies off with her necklace!

"My necklace!" Sofia cries.
She sees marks on the table.
They are from the griffin's claws.

The girls look for the necklace.

Clover, Mia, and Robin want to help.
Sofia cannot understand them.
She needs her necklace for that!

A maid calls for help.
The gold cups are gone.

The thief left marks behind.

"We will find him!" says the guard.

Cedric sees the griffin outside.
It is wearing Sofia's necklace.

Cedric wants the necklace.
It has special magic.

Cedric tries a spell.
It does not work!

Cedric saves his bird.
The griffin gets away.

Cedric tries again.
He puts a shiny jewel in a trap.

"Now we wait," he says.

The griffin is inside the castle.
Sofia's friends see him.
Too bad they cannot tell Sofia.

The griffin has Sofia's necklace.
Clover grabs it.
The griffin will not let go!

Next the griffin takes Cedric's jewel.
The trap does not work.

Cedric grabs for the necklace.
The trap comes down on him!

The queen cannot find her crown.
She sees marks on her table.
She finds a feather, too!

Amber tells her about the other
missing things.

Cedric is still after the griffin.
The griffin loses the jewel.
He loses the crown, too.

Cedric catches them.

Cedric lands in the ballroom.
Everyone sees the jewel and
the crown.

Uh-oh!
They think Cedric took them.

Sofia sees fur and feathers.
She thinks about the claw marks.
Sofia finds the real thief.

The king pets the griffin.

"That tickles!" the griffin says.

Sofia can understand him!

Sofia finds her animal friends.
They have a lot to talk about!